Quack!

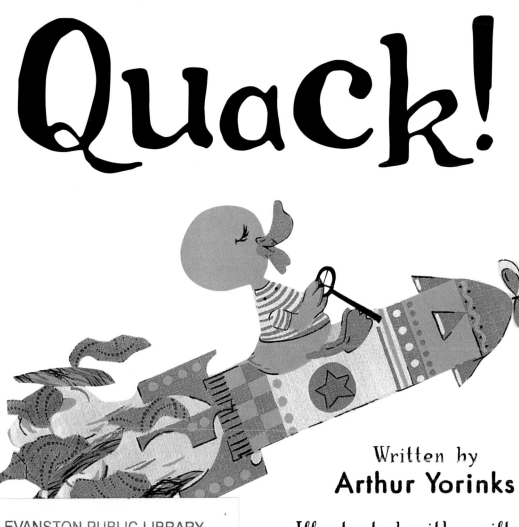

Written by
Arthur Yorinks

Illustrated with quilts by
Adrienne Yorinks

Harry N. Abrams, Inc., Publishers

Quack quack quacked Quack.
Quack quack quack
quack—the moon!

So, Quack quacked quack.

And Quack quacked quack quack quack.

Quack

quack

quack

quack

quack

quack

quack

quack

quack

quack...

QUACK! QUACK!

Quack quack quack quack quack quack quack quack...

Quack quack—the moon!

But the Raccoons quack quack quacked Quack.

And Little Dog quack quack quack quacked Quack.

Even Mrs. Cow quack quack quack quacked Quack.

And the Crocodiles? Quack quacked Quack, too!

Quack quacked quack friends. Quack quacked and quacked.

So Quack quacked!

And quacked

and quacked

and quacked

and quacked

and quacked

and quacked

and quacked...

Artist's Note

I have always loved fabric—all kinds of fabric, from bright cheery patterns to dark moody colors. I collect fabrics from nearly every country that produces it—Africa, Japan, France, India, China, and Italy. I also collect fabrics that are antique; some I have were printed 150 years ago. I love conversational prints, which are fabrics that depict all sorts of objects such as tennis rackets, rocket ships, baseballs, fish, puppy dogs, stars, and of course, ducks. I love fabric so much that I even design my own patterns for a fabric company. All of these fabrics become my palette when I create fabric collage for illustration.

Quack! was inspired by a piece of vintage fabric I found in a thrift store several years ago. It was such a funny piece of fabric with fabulous colors, I thought it would make a wonderful beginning for a book. Arthur and I discussed it, and soon he had a story written in quack. Just as the fabrics sparked my imagination, we hoped that the language would excite children and encourage them to become storytellers by "interpreting" quack to family and friends.

Fabric collage is created by first cutting out patterns or forms (characters), then sewing them together to form a picture. Once the picture, or top of the art, is finished, I place a cotton batting, or filler, underneath it, and a fabric backing beneath the batting. These form a "quilt sandwich," where the top and bottom, or backing, of the quilt is the bread, and the cotton batting in between is like the peanut butter. These three layers need to be held together with top stitches called quilting so they don't fall apart. The quilting stitches create their own pattern on top of the picture. Each little fabric collage is then bound with colorful fabric borders to complete the illustration. In *Quack!*, the combination of vintage fabric and today's brightly colored patterns creates a retro style echoing back to the 1950s.

Designer: Allison Henry
Production Director: Hope Koturo

Library of Congress Cataloging-in-Publication Data

Yorinks, Arthur.
Quack! to the moon and home again / written by Arthur Yorinks; illustrated with quilts by Adrienne Yorinks.
p. cm.
Summary: Quack, a young duck, builds a rocket and goes to the moon, only to find that he misses home.
ISBN 0-8109-3548-1
[1. Ducks—Fiction. 2. Space flight to the moon—Fiction. 3. Animals—Fiction.] I. Yorinks, Adrienne, ill. II. Title.

PZ7.Y815 Qs 2003
[E]—dc21
2002012539

Text copyright © 2003 Arthur Yorinks
Illustrations copyright © 2003 Adrienne Yorinks

Published in 2003 by Harry N. Abrams, Incorporated, New York
All rights reserved. No part of the contents of this book may be
reproduced without the written permission of the publisher.

Printed and bound in China
10 9 8 7 6 5 4 3 2 1

Harry N. Abrams, Inc.
100 Fifth Avenue
New York, N.Y. 10011
www.abramsbooks.com

Abrams is a subsidiary of

LA MARTINIÈRE
GROUPE